Hubby is Hungry

Kosher Everyday Recipes from My Kitchen to Yours

By: Ashira Mirsky

Introduction

When I was a child, I developed a passion for cooking from a very young age. I loved helping my mother in the kitchen, and I looked forward to serving my potato kugel and salads on Shabbos and Yom Tov. Food always came along with fond memories, such as family BBQ's, rolling lokshen for Pesach, and baking chocolate chip cookies for every simcha in the neighborhood. In fact, when I was in high school, the Bais Yaakov PTA came out with a cookbook. And right there, along with the other recipes submitted by the PTA mothers, was a recipe for "Chocolate Chip Cookies by Ashira Mensh." No one could figure out how a teenager managed to get her recipe printed in the book. Initially, I thought it was a prank, yet to this day, people still ask me for my cookie recipe, and we never did figure out who submitted it. In high school, my sisters and I would hold fake "Chopped" competitions in our kitchen on Sundays, with our parents serving as judges. My parents instilled within us a lot of room for experimentation and creativity. I became a third-grade teacher in Bais Yaakov of Baltimore and started to channel my imagination inside of the classroom.

After I got married, my ingenuity in the kitchen began to flourish. I needed a lot of dinner ideas that were quick and easy to prepare, so I started to devise original, uncomplicated recipes. It was around this time that the iPhone came out. (Yup, I feel old). My camera-phone gave me a chance to put my photography skills to the test. After contacting Chumi Friedman, a former editor of The Jewish Press, and emailing her a sample of what I could do, @hubbyishungry was born. My monthly column began in November of 2015, and I've been creating simple and delicious recipes ever since. I also started an Instagram blog,

3

@hubbyishungry, in which I share my recipes and ideas with an ever-growing number of followers. After winning the B'gan's Like It and Win Contest with my tuna tostones recipe, I posted my very first recipe, homemade chicken poppers, on Kosher.com. From there I've continued to grow my recipe box, enjoying hearing from followers who've made recipes from the website. I have been published in the Masbia Rosh Hashanah cookbook, the Chofetz Chaim Heritage Foundation auction booklet, and have made it to the Arutz Sheva and Israel National News pages. I eagerly attend Kosherfest every year to see the hottest new kosher products on the market, and my recipes have been featured for companies such as Gourmet Glatt, MealMart, and De la Rosa.

So why am I telling you all this? To show how a busy wife, mother, and 3rd grade teacher got to the point of publishing this cookbook. In this picture-perfect, social-media obsessed society, I wondered if I could pull off this cookbook without professional lighting, photographers, and props. All the recipes are my own, as well as the photos which were taken on my very own countertops. And you know what? I couldn't be happier with the results. No over-the-top ingredients you can't pronounce, nothing too fancy or too complicated, just really good food that's EASY. It's thanks to you, my loyal followers, who have encouraged me every step of the way to take this next leap in this journey. I want to hear which recipes you cooked at home and which ones are your favorites. I would also like to thank my talented sister, Shoshana Freund of SAM Designs, beamensh@gmail.com. She created the gorgeous cover and graphics throughout the book. I hope you enjoy this cookbook and use it well.

With love from my kitchen to yours,

Ashira Mirsky

In Memory of my Zaidy,

Rabbi Chaim Yitzchok (Howard) Goldman ZT"L

Zaidy, you have left us a beautiful legacy

You infused positivity while taking care of Bubby and our family

We loved to hear Sherlock Holmes stories on your knee.

Your love of Navi and Chumash descended generations

Hot dogs, sweet rolls, soup and compote were always a sensation

You traveled to every simcha with such dedication.

Your cup was always half full, a Sefer constantly in hand

You always had time to help your grandchildren understand...

You were truly a family man. We miss you.

TOP 12 KITCHEN NECESSITIES

The top 12 ingredients I always keep in stock:
(Okay, okay, maybe it's 13 or 14...)

1. **OLIVE OIL**- Thank you to Trader Joe's and Aldi for providing high quality extra virgin olive oil at great prices.

2. **CRUSHED GARLIC**- I happen to love the Dorot crushed garlic that come in cubes in the freezer section. It's so easy to pop out and add to marinades, stir-frys, and whatever you are cooking.

3. **BALSAMIC, RASPBERRY AND POMEGRANATE VINEGAR**- Do not underestimate their power! Chicken, meat, eggrolls, salad dressings...the possibilities are endless and delicious.

4. **WINE**- Red or white, Zmora Cabernet to Rashi or Herzog, it doesn't have to be expensive to enhance a dish. Just remember, whenever pouring some for a recipe, don't forget to pour some for yourself!

5. **TRADER JOE'S EVERYTHING BUT THE BAGEL AND CHILI-LIME SPICES**- No caption necessary.

6. **CHICKEN STOCK**- It enhances everything-meat sauces, rice, soups, etc. It's the easiest shortcut and the best. Freeze your leftover chicken soup or buy it.

7. **HAWAJ AND ZAATAR**- These spices are life. If you have relatives in Israel, ask them to bring some back to America. If not, order online or use brands like Pereg.

8. **SILAN**- It's date syrup. It's a natural way of adding sweetness to dishes, and it doesn't overpower. I love the Galil brand. I even pour it into a squeeze bottle to eliminate a sticky mess. Squeeze on pancakes, yogurt, acai bowls, salads, and more.

9. **ARUGULA**- It's bright green, tastes fresh, peppery and crunchy. Goodbye, wilted romaine lettuce. It also always adds visual appeal.

10. **GOAT CHEESE**- Subtle flavor, but big impact. Use in quiches, shakshuka, or anything dairy. You will thank me.

11. **COCONUT MILK-** Creamy, Parve, and delicious. It makes a great addition to soups, desserts and chicken curry. For those of you who are coconut haters, the flavor is so subtle you'll hardly even know it's there!

12. **SEA SALT-** Tastes saltier than regular table salt, but so delicious. Sea salt comes in flaky and regular varieties and adds flavor in all dishes.

TABLE OF CONTENTS

11 Soups

23 Salads

35 Apps & Mains

73 Dairy & Drinks

93 Sides

105 Desserts

Soups

Winter Soup

Servings: 5-6

Prep Time: 10 minutes

Cook Time: 1 hour

Ingredients:

1 bag frozen Pardes Farms winter mix (cauliflower and broccoli)

2 Yukon gold potatoes

1 onion

3 frozen Dorot garlic cubes

32 oz. vegetable stock (I use Manischewitz)

2 c. water

1 tsp. dried dill

Salt and pepper

1 bay leaf

2 tsp. avocado oil

Directions:

1. Sauté the onions in avocado oil along with the garlic cubes. Add the bag of frozen veggies and continue to sauté for a few minutes. Peel and dice the potatoes and add them to the pot.
2. Season with generous amounts of salt and pepper. Add the dill and bay leaf. Pour the veggie stock and water to cover and bring to a boil.
3. Simmer for 45 minutes to 1 hour, then take out the bay leaf. Blend with an immersion blender. Enjoy!

Winter Soup

Hawaj French Onion Soup & Cheesy Toasts

Serves: 4-6

Prep Time: 10 min.

Cook Time: 40 min.

Ingredients:

7 medium sized onions

2 Tbsp. salted butter

salt and pepper

1 tsp. Hawaj seasoning

½ tsp. thyme

1 ½ c. white wine

1 heaping tbsp. onion soup mix (I use Osem)

1 Tbsp. silan

2 Tbsp. flour

Bagel chips plus cheese

Directions:

1. Dice the onions. In a large pot, sauté the onions in butter for around 10 minutes, stirring constantly until evenly browned. Add the thyme, Hawaj, silan, and generous amounts of salt and pepper.
2. Add the white wine to the pot to deglaze. Cook for a few minutes until the alcohol has cooked out. Add the flour to the pot on the flame and continue to stir until a thick brown onion mixture has formed.
3. At this point, fill the pot halfway with water. Add some more salt to season. Cover and let the pot simmer on low for 35-40 min.
4. Take bagel chips and Muenster cheese. Toast in the toaster oven for a few minutes until cheese has melted. Float the crisps on top of the soup.

Hawaj French Onion Soup

Creamy Cauliflower Potato Leek Soup with Homemade Croutons

Servings: 6

Prep Time: 10 min

Cook Time: 50 min.

Ingredients:

2 big onions

3 frozen garlic cubes such as Dorot

1 leek

2 Yukon Gold potatoes

1 bag of frozen cauliflower

Tabachnick or similar box of chicken stock

olive oil

salt and pepper

Croutons:

Dice up pitas, bread or rolls- drizzle with olive oil, salt, garlic powder and paprika

Bake on a baking sheet at 400 until crispy

Directions:

1. Add olive oil to a big pot. Dice the onions and sauté with garlic until golden brown.
2. Dice up the whole leek into small bits and add to the pot.
3. Cube the peeled potatoes & add to the pot along with the bag of cauliflower. Keep sautéing everything in the pot for about 10 minutes, until golden.
4. Slowly add your box of chicken stock. Add salt and pepper to your taste. Lower the flame and cook for around 50 minutes.
   Take off the fire and puree. If the soup
5. is too thick, add some more stock to thin it out. Make some homemade croutons for an added crunch. Enjoy!

Cauliflower Soup

Minestrone Soup

Servings: 4-6

Prep Time: 10 min.

Cook Time: 50 min.

Ingredients:

2 stalks celery, diced

1 large onion

2 large carrots, diced

1 summer squash, diced

1 Tbsp. butter or margarine

salt and pepper

2 heaping Tbsp. Leiber's salad spice

(a mixture of oregano, paprika, parsley, garlic powder, salt and sugar)

3 Tbsp. tomato paste

32 oz. vegetable stock

3 cups water

1 c. gigli pasta (I use Trader Joe's)

Directions:

1. Sauté the diced onion, carrots, squash and celery with the margarine or butter in a large soup pot. Add the salad spice and salt and pepper. Add the tomato paste to the veggies. Fill the pot with stock and water.
2. Simmer on low for about an hour. In last ten minutes, add 1 cup of pasta to the soup. Cook until the pasta is done. Enjoy with crusty bread.

Minestrone Soup

Creamy Carrot Coconut Soup with Parsnip Curls

Servings: 6-8

Prep Time: 10 min.

Cook Time: 50 min.

Ingredients:

1 large onion	3 c. water
3 stalks celery, diced	1 can coconut milk
4 large carrots, diced	1 tsp. Lawry's garlic salt
2 large sweet potatoes, diced	
1 box (32 oz.) chicken or veggie stock	

Parsnip Curls:

3-4 large parsnips

sea salt and pepper

olive oil

Spiralizer (Available on Amazon)

Directions:

1. Sauté the onion, celery, carrots and sweet potatoes in some olive oil in a big pot. Add garlic salt. Add the box of stock and water to the pot. Bring to a boil, then simmer on low for 45 min.
2. Meanwhile, spiralize the parsnips. Spread the curls out on a baking sheet, and toss lightly with olive oil, sea salt and pepper. Bake at 400 for 20-25 min. or until roasted.
3. Blend the finished soup with an immersion blender. While still hot, add the can of coconut milk. Continue to blend another minute until creamy.
4. Top the creamy soup with roasted parsnip curls.

Carrot Coconut Soup
With Parsnip Curls

Salads

Summer Slaw

Servings: 4

Prep time: 20 min.

Ingredients:

1 14 oz. bag of coleslaw

1 c. red cabbage

1 c. roasted broccoli

¼ c. cooked quinoa

¼ c. sunflower seeds

Vinaigrette:

¼ c. olive oil

¼ c. De La Rosa raspberry vinegar

1 fresh lemon

2 heaping Tbsp. maple syrup

Directions:

1. Set out the broccoli on a baking sheet. Drizzle with olive oil and salt and cook on 425 for about 15 minutes until roasted. Meanwhile, cook the quinoa and let it cool.
2. Whisk the De La Rosa vinegar and olive oil with the maple syrup. Squeeze the lemon into the vinaigrette and mix well.
3. In a bowl, combine the coleslaw, red cabbage, broccoli, quinoa and sunflower seeds. Pour the vinaigrette over the slaw and enjoy!

Summer Slaw

Skirt Steak Salad with Creamy Pesto Dressing

Servings: 2-4

Prep Time: 45 min.

Cook Time: 5 min.

Ingredients:

1.5 lb skirt steak

1 can coconut milk

Juice of 1 orange

A shake of dried ginger

Spring Mix lettuce, grape tomatoes, sliced cucumbers

Dressing:

¼ bag sliced almonds

3 frozen garlic cubes

1 bunch fresh parsley

2 tsp. dried basil

2 tsp mayo

2 tsp sugar

2 heaping tsp mayo

3 tsp. apple cider vinegar

1 c. olive oil

1/8 c. water

Directions:

1. In a food processor, blend the garlic, almonds, parsley and basil until a fine paste forms. Add the apple cider vinegar, mayo, and slowly drizzle in olive oil. Add the water, and if it's too thick, add some more water. Refrigerate the dressing until ready to serve.
2. Rinse the steaks well and pat them dry. Place the steaks in a ziploc bag and pour in a can of

coconut milk. Add the ginger to the bag and squeeze the orange. Let the steaks rest for 40 minutes. This will eliminate some of the salt and add a depth of flavor. Once marinated, pat the steaks dry and grill on a hot grill pan for 1-2 minutes per side. Serve the grilled skirt steak over a bed of lettuce, tomatoes and cucumbers and drizzle the pesto dressing on top. Enjoy!

Skirt Steak Salad

Quinoa Salad

Servings: 6

Prep Time: 5 min.

Cook Time: 15 min.

Ingredients:

2 c. quinoa

4 c. water

2 sprigs checked mint

1 bunch scallions

1 box heirloom tomatoes

2 Tbsp. olive oil

2 Tbsp. silan

2 Tbsp. balsamic vinegar

salt and pepper

Directions:

1. Cook the quinoa according to package directions. Let cool.
2. Cut the mint and scallions and halve the heirloom tomatoes. Mix with the quinoa.
3. Drizzle the olive oil, vinegar, silan, salt and pepper over the quinoa. Serve cold or at room temperature.

Quinoa Salad

Grilled Chicken Salad with Tahini Vinaigrette

Servings: 2-4

Prep Time: 15 min.

Cook Time: 5-7 min.

Ingredients:

1 package boneless chicken

1 tsp. oregano

1 tsp. garlic powder

¼ c. olive oil

¼ c. balsamic vinegar

Romaine lettuce, cherry tomatoes, cucumbers

1 XL sweet potato

Dressing:

1 Tbsp. tahini

½ c. balsamic vinegar

½ c. olive oil

2 heaping Tbsp. honey

Directions:

1. Marinate the chicken in the olive oil, balsamic, oregano and garlic. Dice the sweet potato, spray with canola oil, season with salt and pepper. Bake on 400 until fully cooked. Grill the chicken for a few minutes a side. Serve the grilled chicken over the lettuce, tomatoes, cucumbers and roasted sweet potatoes.
2. Combine the dressing ingredients and shake well. Serve on top of the salad.

Grilled Chicken Salad
With Tahini Vinaigrette

Sometimes, I let the ingredients shine on their own. Heirloom tomatoes in the summer become one of those times! This bright, crunchy, fresh and delicious salad is simple and satisfying served with any meal. I often make it on Friday nights to accompany heavy meat or chicken.

Heirloom Tomato Salad

Servings: 4

Prep Time: 5 min.

Ingredients:

2 pints heirloom tomatoes

1 bunch scallions

2 Tbsp. olive oil

2 tsp. balsamic vinegar

½ tsp. Lawry's garlic salt

½ tsp. garlic powder

½ tsp. soy sauce

Directions:

1. Slice the tomatoes in half and place into a bowl. Slice the scallions and scatter on top.
2. Mix the dressing ingredients and pour over the salad.

Heirloom Tomato Salad

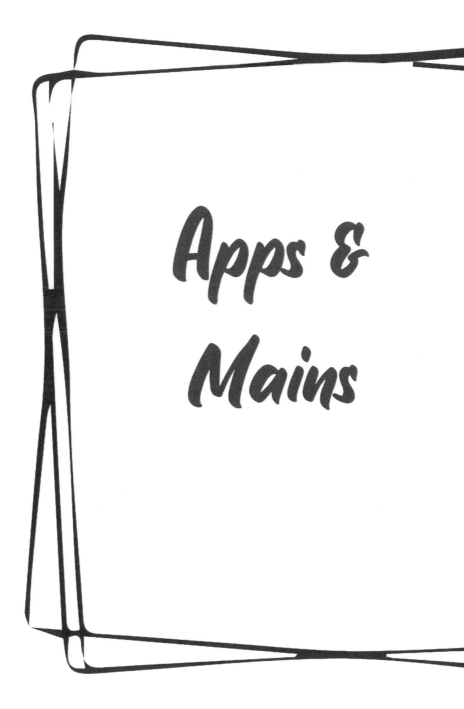

Apps & Mains

I don't know about you, but I have a little pan-phobia. What is pan-phobia, you may ask? A phobia of making a dish that calls for too many bowls, saucepans, and utensils that need washing afterwards. I'm constantly looking for shortcuts to keep my kitchen clean. (For example, mixing things in a 9 by 13 pan and then throwing it away afterwards- best hack of life!) I love Lo Mein, but don't want a two-pot mess. I decided to play around with a thick sauce and raw noodles, and I came up with the perfect, no-fail, one pan Lo Mein!

One Pan Chicken Lo Mein

Servings: 4

Prep Time: 10 min.

Cook Time: 20 min.

Ingredients:

2 tablespoons sesame oil

2 cubes frozen grated ginger (I used Dorot)

½ bag frozen broccoli florets

1 package chicken fingers or cubed boneless chicken

6 oz. bag of snow peas

1 bunch of scallions

3 heaping cups of chicken stock

½ c. soy sauce

½ c. creamy smooth peanut butter

3 tsp. brown sugar

1 Tbsp. dried ground mustard

½ tsp. crushed red pepper flakes

Sesame seeds

¾ of a 12 oz. bag of medium egg noodles (I used Manischewitz)

Directions:

1. In a bowl, whisk together the chicken stock, peanut butter, soy sauce, brown sugar, dried mustard, red pepper flakes,

and sliced scallions. Reserve some scallions for garnishing at the end. In a large skillet, sauté the chicken strips in sesame oil until done. Add the broccoli and ginger cubes and continue to sauté until fully cooked.

2. Pour the sauce over the chicken and broccoli mixture. Bring to a boil. Add the raw egg noodles directly into the pan. Cover the pan and cook 4-5 minutes until the egg noodles have softened and are coated in the sauce. The starches from the egg noodles will thicken the sauce. Add the snow peas to the Lo Mein. Top with remaining scallions and sesame seeds.

One Pan Chicken Lo Mein

I'm famous for my pastrami eggrolls. You know that nut that spends her entire Purim hand-pinching 85 eggrolls? That's me. This is my usual dish that I volunteer to bring to the Purim Seudah each year, because everybody looks forward to eating them. It's my number one most requested recipe. You can either bake or fry the eggrolls with the same results. Enjoy!

Pastrami Eggrolls with Apricot dipping sauce

Servings: 6-8

Prep Time: 10 min.

Cook Time: 12-14 min.

Ingredients:

3 onions, diced

bunch of scallions

1 ½ lb. pastrami or turkey pastrami

Eggroll/Wonton wrappers

3 Tbsps. brown sugar

4 Tbsps. balsamic vinegar

Dipping sauce:

1 jar apricot jelly

1 tsp. garlic powder

1 tsp. onion powder

¼ c. balsamic vinegar

1 tsp. soy sauce

Directions:

1. Sauté the onions. Cube the sliced pastrami and add it to the pan and sauté until crispy. Add the balsamic vinegar and brown sugar. Add the diced scallions at the end.
2. Wet each edge of the eggroll wrapper before filling and rolling them up. This will help the edges stick together. Lay them flat on a greased cookie sheet and bake in the oven at 400 degrees for about 12-14 minutes, until golden and crispy.
3. To make the dipping sauce, add the ingredients to a small saucepan. Boil a few minutes, then let cool before serving. Garnish with scallions. Enjoy!

Pastrami Eggrolls
With apricot dipping sauce

This chicken is Kosher for Pesach but is very much enjoyed all year long. It's like a marsala, but sweet and savory. I chose this recipe for the cover because it stands for the theme of this book: fresh, easy, and flavorful. Add this to your Friday night menu to impress your guests!

Balsamic Mushroom Chicken

Servings: 4-6

Prep Time: 15 min.

Cooking Time: 1 hour, 40 min.

Ingredients:

1 package of chicken thighs

8 oz. container of baby portobello mushrooms

1 large onion

2 cloves minced garlic

1 c. white wine

¼ c. balsamic vinegar

¼ c. silan

salt and pepper

Directions:

1. Preheat the oven to 400. Sauté the chicken thighs, skin side down, in olive oil until crispy. Flip to other side, then remove.
2. In the same pan, sauté the onions, mushrooms and garlic. Add the Silan and balsamic vinegar. Add the white wine and cook for a few more minutes.
3. Add the chicken back to the pan and baste with the juices. Cover and transfer to the oven. Bake for one hour covered, and 15 minutes uncovered.

Balsamic Mushroom Chicken

Pesto Pappardelle with Blistered Tomatoes and Salmon

Servings: 4

Prep Time: 10 min.

Cook Time: 25 min.

Ingredients:

4 salmon fillets

1 package pappardelle

1 box grape tomatoes

1 cube crushed garlic

4 teaspoons apple cider vinegar

Trader Joe's Chile Lime Seasoning

1 oz. checked basil leaves

1 bunch of checked parsley

1 c. walnuts

2 cubes of crushed garlic

½ c. olive oil

salt, to taste

Silan

Directions:

1. In a food processor, blend the walnuts, two cubes of crushed garlic, basil, parsley and olive oil until pesto forms. Store in an airtight container in the fridge for up to a week or so. Great to use on meat, chicken or fish.
2. Preheat the oven to 400. Spray a pan with cooking spray and place the salmon fillets in the pan. Pour one teaspoon of apple cider vinegar over each fillet. Pour generous amounts of chili lime spice and Silan over the fish. Bake for 25 minutes.
3. Coat a nonstick skillet with a little olive oil. Add the package of cherry tomatoes, some salt, and a cube of crushed garlic. Cook on a low flame for 5-10 minutes until the tomatoes start to open and blister.

4. Cook the pappardelle according to package directions and drain. Toss with ¼ cup pesto. Add the blistered cherry tomatoes to the pasta. Place the salmon on top. Enjoy!

Pesto Pappardelle
with blistered tomatoes and salmon

It's Chanukah 2020, and I've been dreaming up a new latke recipe that is modern, beautiful and contemporary. This recipe is versatile, delicious and can be served for breakfast, lunch or supper. I happen to love beets, and what is more exciting than a purple latke? Even my three-year-old ventured to try one. The crunchy arugula, pesto drizzle and runny egg elevate this dish to extraordinary!

Purple Latkes Supreme

Servings: 4-6

Prep Time: 10 min.

Cooking Time: 10 min.

Ingredients:

1 XXL purple sweet potato

1 small onion

2 Gefen beets

2 eggs

3 tablespoons flour

salt and pepper

Canola Oil

1 bunch of checked arugula

Pesto Dressing:

2 tsp. mayo

2 tsp. pesto (store-bought or homemade)

1 tsp. silan

2 tsp. water

1-2 eggs, cooked sunny-side up

squeeze bottle

Directions:

1. In a food processor, shred the purple sweet potato, beets, and onion. Pour the mixture into a big bowl, and mix in the eggs, salt, pepper, and flour. Pour some oil in a non-stick skillet, and when hot, drop large spoonfuls of batter into the oil. Cook until crispy on both sides, then drain on a paper towel.

2. Mix the pesto dressing ingredients together in a cup. Pour into a squeeze bottle for a nice effect.
3. Cook some eggs sunny-side up style. Layer the latkes, arugula, eggs, and squeeze pesto drizzle on top. Enjoy!

Purple Latkes

Maple Dijon Chicken

Servings: 4-6

Prep Time: 10 min.

Cook Time: 1 hour and 45 min.

Ingredients:

1 package of chicken thighs

1 large onion, diced

¼ c. Dijon mustard

¼ c. maple syrup

¼ c. olive oil

salt & pepper

fresh checked rosemary

Directions:

1. Dice the onion and spread on the bottom of an aluminum or roasting pan. Place the thighs on top.
2. Whisk the mustard, olive oil, maple syrup, and salt and pepper together in a bowl. Pour over the chicken. Throw in a few fresh sprigs of rosemary.
3. Cover tightly with foil and bake at 400 for 1 hour and 45 minutes. Uncover for the last 10 minutes. Garnish with fresh rosemary. Enjoy!

Maple Dijon Chicken

When my hubby said on a date that Dougie's fried chicken poppers were his favorite food, I nodded and smiled and thought to myself that those days are now done. But the catch is- those days have yet to be over! Although Hubby enjoys all my recipes tremendously, there is still something that attracts men to hot poppers, much like women to shopping. I decided to create a homemade version which is on the healthy(ish) side because it's not fried, and it's not greasy takeout.

Baked Poppers

Servings: 5

Prep Time: 10 min.

Cook Time: 30 min.

Ingredients:

1 package of boneless chicken (cut up into cubes)

2 c. flour

2 eggs

3-4 c. crushed cornflakes (I used the cereal and crushed it by hand for a thicker consistency)

¼ c. Frank's hot sauce

2 c. dark brown sugar

2 tsp. canola oil

1 c. ketchup

Directions:

1. Dredge each piece of chicken in flour, then egg, then crushed cornflakes, and place in a 9 by 13 pan.
2. Spray the tops of the chicken nuggets well with cooking spray and bake at 425 for 20 minutes until golden and crispy.
3. Meanwhile, mix the ketchup, oil, brown sugar and hot sauce. Pour over the cooked nuggets and bake for an additional ten minutes.

Baked Poppers

I took lamb "bacon" and paired it with cubes of lamb and beef from my local butcher to create marinated kebabs. Alternatively, you can use this recipe with baby chicken, as well. The kebabs were bursting with flavor but needed something starchy as a side. Quinoa is a great alternative to rice, mashed potatoes, or noodles. It's gluten-free, a superfood, and quite easy to cook. Not only is it good for you, but it tastes good, too.

Lamb Kebabs with Roasted Veggie Quinoa

Servings: 2

Prep Time: 4-5 hours

Cook Time: 5 min.

Ingredients:

1 package lamb "bacon"

1 lb. beef cubes

1 lb. lamb cubes

cherry tomatoes

1 c. olive oil

fresh sage

5 tsps. soy sauce

4 crushed garlic cubes

salt and pepper

4 tsps. lemon juice

metal skewers

Directions:

1. Plan and assemble your kebabs a few hours before eating. Take a metal skewer, and layer lamb 'bacon," cubes of lamb, chicken, or beef, and cherry tomatoes, and repeat.
2. Whisk together 1 c. olive oil, salt and pepper, lemon juice, soy sauce, and crushed garlic. Cut up the sage leaves and add that to the mix.
3. Pour the marinade over the kebabs in a big plastic bag. Let the kebabs sit in the marinade for at least five hours. Then, grill your kebabs to your liking or broil in the oven on a baking sheet until crispy and browned.

Lamb Kebabs

Sous Vide Flank Steak with Mango Pesto aka *"Summer on a board"*

Servings: 4

Prep Time: 2 hours

Cook Time: 20 Min.

Ingredients:

1.5 lb. flank steak

salt and pepper

fresh thyme, rosemary or parsley

Pesto:

3 garlic cloves

1 bunch of fresh parsley

½ bag slivered almonds

1 cup extra virgin olive oil

1 tsp. white vinegar

1 ripe mango

Sides:

1 head of fresh bok choy

salt, pepper, and extra virgin olive oil

small fingerling potatoes (I use Trader Joe's)

1 shallot

Directions:

1. Place the flank steak in a Ziploc bag with salt, pepper, and aromatics. Sous vide on 132 F for a medium-well steak for two hours.
2. Meanwhile, make the pesto. Coarsely chop the garlic and slivered almonds in a food processor. Add the parsley, vinegar, and olive oil. Dice the mango into small cubes. Add half and pulse for a few more seconds and add the second half into the pesto with a spoon and mix by hand.
3. Pat the steak dry, season again, and grill for a few minutes on each side

until charred and brown. Let the steak rest for a few minutes before cutting it.

4. Serve the steak with the mango pesto on the side or on top. Grill the bok choy for a few minutes on each side, while drizzling with a little olive oil and seasoning with salt and pepper. Slice the fingerling potatoes in half and top with diced shallots on a baking sheet. Drizzle with olive oil, salt, and pepper and bake on 400 until ready. Serve the sides with the steak. Enjoy!

Sous Vide Flank Steak with Mango Pesto

Best Brisket

Prep Time: 10 min.

Cook Time: 3-4 hours

Ingredients:

4 lb. second cut brisket   1 bottle Zmora cabernet

1 c. duck sauce   5 frozen garlic cubes

½ c. onion soup mix   1 large onion, diced

Directions:

1. Preheat the oven to 350. Place the diced onions and garlic cubes on the bottom of a large roasting pan. Add the meat on top. Smother the meat with the duck sauce and onion soup mix. Pour half the bottle of wine on top. Season with salt and pepper.
2. Cover tightly and place in the oven. Bake covered for 3-4 hours or until the meat is extremely soft. Slice against the grain.

BBQ Pulled Chicken

Prep Time: 3 min.

Cook Time: 4-5 hours

Ingredients:

1 package of boneless chicken   ½ c. BBQ sauce

½ c. salsa   ½ c. duck sauce

Directions:

3. Pour sauces over chicken in the crockpot. Cook on low for 4-5 hours until tender enough to shred. Pull with a fork.
4. If the sauce is too thin, add a slurry of a little cornstarch mixed with water to the crockpot. Pour it back in and cook for an additional 5 minutes on low. Stir until the sauce thickens.

Best Brisket

BBQ Pulled Chicken

Pulled BBQ Beef Flatbread

Servings: 2 flatbreads

Prep Time: 4-5 hours

Cook Time: 15 min.

Ingredients:

2 lb. second cut brisket

package of flatbreads (I used Trader Joe's)

1/3 c. BBQ sauce

1/3 c. coarse ground mustard

1/3 c. ketchup

1 c. sweet white wine (such as Rashi)

1 box arugula

2 large onions

1 jar marinara sauce

Spicy Mayo (I use Lieber's)

Directions:

1. Place your meat in a crockpot. Pour over the wine, BBQ sauce, ketchup and mustard. Let it cook on low for 4-5 hours or until tender enough to shred. Pull the meat with a fork.
2. Sauté the onions in some olive oil until browned. On the flatbreads, spread a thin layer of marinara sauce and sautéed onions. Top with the pulled beef. Bake on a cookie sheet at 400 for 10-15 min. to crisp up.
3. Top with fresh arugula and spicy mayo. Enjoy!

Pulled BBQ Beef Flatbread

Chinese "Takeout" Chicken

Servings: 6

Prep Time: 5 min.

Cook Time: 15 min.

Ingredients:

1 large onion, diced

2 orange or yellow peppers, diced

1 package boneless chicken fingers

1 Tbsp. Worcestershire sauce

1 Tbsp. Teriyaki sauce

¼ c. dark brown sugar

¼ c. soy sauce

1 heaping tsp. cornstarch dissolved in ½ c. water

sesame seeds

scallions, for garnish

Directions:

1. Sauté the onions and peppers in a little olive oil until cooked through. Remove from pan. Add the chicken and sauté until fully cooked. Add the veggies back to pan, along with the soy sauce, teriyaki sauce, brown sugar and Worcestershire sauce. Continue to cook on a low flame for a few more minutes.
2. Add the cornstarch slurry to the pan. Continue to mix until the sauce has thickened. Generously sprinkle sesame seeds and sliced scallions on top.

Chinese "Takeout" Chicken

BBQ Beef Empanadas with Avocado Aioli

Servings: 5

Prep Time: 10 min.

Cook Time: 20 min.

Ingredients:

Pulled Beef (recipe on page 56)

1 package empanada wrappers (I use Goya)

Avocado Aioli:

1 ripe avocado

3 heaping tsps. light mayo

1 Tbsp. lemon juice

1 small garlic clove

garlic salt, to taste

2 tsp. olive oil

2 Tbsp. water

Directions:

1. Preheat oven to 425 degrees. Take an empanada dough wrapper and fill with a tablespoon of shredded beef. Pinch the corners tight with a fork and place on a baking sheet. Brush each one with an egg wash.
2. Bake for 15–20 minutes or until golden brown

For the Avocado Aioli:

1. In a blender or food processor, blend the aioli ingredients. If it's too thick, add some more water to thin it out. Pour into a squeeze bottle and serve as a condiment alongside the empanadas. Enjoy!

BBQ Beef Empanadas

*One of my favorite go-to dishes is my succulent chicken
with squash recipe. I am so excited to be able to share this recipe
with you. I make this one-pan dish for Friday nights, Rosh Hashanah,
or Sukkos. It's super easy, looks gorgeous, and has all the fall and
winter "feels." Kids and adults both love it.*

Succulent Chicken with Squash

Servings: 6

Prep Time: 10 min.

Cook Time: 2 hours and 45 min.

Ingredients:

1 package of chicken cut into 1/8ths

2 large shallots

1 butternut squash

3 Tbsp. stone-ground mustard

3 Tbsp. red wine vinegar

1 Tbsp. De La Rosa raspberry vinegar

3 Tbsp. maple syrup

2 Tbsp. olive oil

1 tsp. dried rosemary

2 tsp. crushed garlic

salt and pepper

fresh parsley, for garnish

Directions:

1. Dice the shallots and the butternut squash. Place in the bottom of a large roasting pan. Place the chicken on top, and season with salt and pepper.
2. In a mixing bowl, whisk the mustard, vinegars, maple syrup, olive oil, garlic and rosemary. Pour over the chicken and squash. Cover the roasting pan and cook on 400 for two hours.
3. Uncover after two hours and baste the chicken with the juices. Continue to cook for 45 minutes uncovered, or until the chicken is glossy and well-done. Enjoy!

Succulent Chicken with Squash

I just made the best short ribs ever. I'm not kidding. Ribs are one of my favorite foods. They are juicy, full of favor, and succulent. I have great memories of eating huge dinosaur ribs with Hubby at Milt's in Chicago and at Fuego in Miami. The key is slow-roasting the ribs in the oven at a low temperature. This makes them fall-off the bone delectable and oh-so-good.

Tangy Short Ribs

Servings: 4

Prep Time: 5 min

Cook Time: 3- 3.5 hours

Ingredients:

1 onion

3-4 short ribs

1/2 c. ketchup

1/4 c. BBQ sauce

1 cup apple juice

½ c. duck sauce

3 garlic cloves

2 heaping Tbsp. onion soup mix

2 heaping Tbsp. soy sauce

1 large orange

Directions:

1. Cut the onion and orange and place on the bottom of a pan with the garlic cloves. Mix the rest of the ingredients and pour over the ribs.
2. Cover the pan tightly with foil and bake at 325 for three hours. The ribs will be succulent, soft, and falling off the bone tender. Enjoy!

Tangy Short Ribs

Sweet and Sour Salmon

Servings: 4

Prep time: 15 min.

Cook time: 35 min.

Ingredients:

4 salmon fillets

2 Tbsp. avocado oil

2 red onions

1 fresh lemon

1/3 c. coconut palm sugar or brown sugar

1/4 c. pomegranate vinegar or balsamic vinegar

Directions:

1. Preheat the oven to 375.
2. Drizzle the avocado oil into a frying pan on a low heat. Cut the red onions into small slivers and sauté until golden browned, for about 6-7 minutes. Add the coconut palm sugar to the sautéed onions, along with the pomegranate vinegar. Let the onions cook in the sweet and sour glaze for another five minutes. They should turn a gorgeous dark purple caramelized color.
3. Arrange the salmon fillets in a pan. Squeeze the juice of a fresh lemon on top of the fillets. Top the fish with the caramelized sweet and sour onion mixture. Bake at 375 for 30-35 minutes uncovered. Enjoy!

Sweet & Sour Salmon

Cilantro Pesto Tacos

Servings: 6

Prep Time: 1 hour

Cook Time: 8-10 min.

Ingredients:

1 package soft flour tortillas

1 package boneless chicken

1 bag coleslaw

2 limes

3 fresh corn on the cobs

1 bunch checked cilantro

½ c. walnuts

1 1/2 c. olive oil

1 Tbsp. garlic powder

salt and pepper

Directions:

1. In a food processor, blend the cilantro, walnuts, olive oil, garlic powder, salt and pepper. Take out one cup of pesto and reserve for the slaw.
2. Pour the remaining pesto over the chicken and marinate in the fridge for an hour or more.
3. Grill the chicken and the tacos. Cut the fresh corn off the cob and add to the slaw. Toss the slaw with the pesto and juice of two fresh limes.
4. Serve the taco open-faced with the slaw and grilled chicken on top.

Cilantro Pesto Tacos

Who eats a plain BLT when you could have a BCBG? That's like saying you're going to opt for the Corolla at the car rental place when you could get a convertible. The creamy savory green sauce, sweet bacon, and toasted bun make this the ULTIMATE sandwich.

The BCBG (Bacon, Chicken, on a Toasted Bun with a Green Goddess Sauce)

Servings: 6

Prep Time: 20 min.

Cook Time: 20 min.

Ingredients:

1 package flattened boneless chicken

1 bottle Italian dressing

1 package ciabatta buns

1 tomato, sliced thin

1 package kosher beef bacon

2 Tbsp. light brown sugar

A few romaine leaves

Green Goddess Sauce:

1 avocado

¼ c. mayo

¼ c. fresh cilantro

1 garlic cube

1 lemon

1 tsp. garlic salt

Directions:

1. Marinate the chicken in the Italian dressing and grill. Toast the buns on the grill, as well.

2. Sprinkle the bacon with the brown sugar and lay flat on a cookie sheet. Bake on 425 for 10 min. until crispy.
3. Blend the avocado, cilantro, mayo, garlic cube, juice of a lemon, and salt in the food processer.
4. Spread the Green Goddess sauce on a toasted bun and layer the chicken, tomato, lettuce and bacon on top.

The BCBG

Dairy & Drinks

1-2-3 Shakshuka

Servings: 3-4

Prep Time: 5 min.

Cook Time: 15 min.

Ingredients:

1 jar Gefen Pasta or Pizza Sauce

3 bell peppers, diced

1 large tomato, diced

1 large yellow onion, diced

2 cubes crushed garlic

1 bunch of checked parsley

5 eggs

salt and pepper

1 avocado

shredded cheese

crusty bread

Directions:

1. In a large sauté pan, sauté the garlic and diced onions and peppers. Add the fresh parsley. Season with salt and pepper.
2. Pour the marinara sauce over the sautéed veggies and continue to cook for a few minutes.
3. Crack your eggs directly into the pan and cover loosely. Continue to cook for an additional 5 minutes until the egg whites have set.
4. Top the shakshuka with diced avocado and shredded cheese. Serve with crusty bread.

1-2-3Shakshuka

Cheddar Heirloom Tomato Tart

Servings: 4

Prep Time: 10 min.

Cook Time: 25 min.

Ingredients:

1 package of phyllo dough

½ stick of butter, melted

½ bag shredded cheddar cheese

1-pint colorful heirloom tomatoes

2 heaping Tbsp. whipped cream cheese

2 heaping Tbsp. light mayo

chopped fresh scallions

2-3 fresh basil leaves, chopped

salt, pepper, and garlic powder to taste

Directions:

1. Brush each piece of phyllo dough with melted butter. Stack about 10 pieces on top of each other and lay flat on a baking sheet to form a crust. Preheat the oven to 425. Mix the cream cheese, with the mayo, spices and herbs. Spread on the phyllo dough, leaving 1/2 an inch border as a crust.
2. Cut the heirloom tomatoes in half, salt them, and lay out on paper towels to drain. Pat the tomatoes dry of excess juices, then arrange in a pretty pattern on top of the cream cheese mixture. Top with some extra salt and pepper and bake for about 25 minutes or until golden brown and crispy. Enjoy!

Cheddar Heirloom Tomato Tart

Ravioli in Cream Sauce with Summer Squash and Tomatoes

Servings: 4

Prep Time: 15 min.

Cook Time: 10 min.

Ingredients:

1 package frozen cheese ravioli

1 Tbsp. salted butter

1 Tbsp. flour

1/2 c. whole milk

1 c. cheddar cheese

salt and pepper

1 yellow squash

1 shallot

1 bunch of checked basil

1-pint cherry tomatoes

Directions:

1. Cook the ravioli pasta al dente. In a sauté pan, lightly sauté the shallots, halved tomatoes, diced squash and torn basil in some butter. Set aside.
2. In a saucepan, make a roux. Melt the butter and the flour and whisk until crumbs form. Slowly add milk while continuing to whisk over the heat into a thick sauce. Add generous amounts of salt and pepper, and 1 c. shredded cheddar cheese. If the sauce is too thick, add some more milk.
3. Toss the pasta in the sauce and add the sautéed veggies. Top with more basil.

Ravioli in Cream Sauce

Tuna Tostones

Servings: 6

Prep Time: 10 min.

Cook Time: 10 min.

Ingredients:

2 fresh tuna steaks

1 bag frozen tostones

2 avocados

1 red onion

1 big tomato

1 cup teriyaki sauce

black and white sesame seeds

2 limes

1 bunch checked cilantro

1 c. sour cream

1-2 Tbsp. heavy cream

Salt and pepper

Directions:

1. Fry the tostones according to the package directions. Mash the avocados, add a diced tomato, a diced red onion, salt to taste, and a splash of lime juice.
2. Cube the tuna and marinate it in teriyaki sauce for a few minutes. Then roll each piece of tuna in black and white sesame seeds.
3. Grill the tuna on a greased grill pan for a few minutes on each side. The outside should be well done while the inside remains rare. Spread the guacamole on each tostone and top with a piece of tuna.
4. Mix the sour cream, heavy cream, and juice from half a lime in a bowl. Transfer the crema into a squeeze bottle and squeeze it on top of your tuna tostones. Garnish with fresh cilantro.

Tuna Tostones

Baja Fish Tacos

Servings: 4

Prep Time: 10 min.

Cook Time: 10 min.

Ingredients:

1 package of tortillas

1 package frozen tilapia fillets

1 fresh lemon

1 tsp. Trader Joe's chili-lime spice

1 tsp. paprika

1 tsp. garlic powder

1 ½ c. flour

12 oz. beer

1 bag coleslaw

oil and vinegar

juice of an orange

1 avocado

Baja Sauce:

1 c. mayo

1 c. sour cream

1 lime

1 bunch fresh cilantro

1 tsp. dried dill

Directions:

1. Defrost the tilapia, then cut into bite size pieces. Squeeze some fresh lemon on top of the fish. Sprinkle the garlic powder, paprika and chili lime spice. Mix the flour and beer together to make the beer batter.
2. Pat the fish fillets dry, coat in the beer batter, and then fry in canola oil until crispy and golden. Let the fried fish drain on a paper towel.
3. Make the Baja sauce by mixing the sour cream, mayo, some chopped cilantro, dill, and the juice of a lime.
4. Mix the slaw with the juice of an orange and oil and vinegar of your choice. Top a grilled taco with Baja sauce, fish, slaw, and diced avocado.

Baja Fish Tacos

Pomegranate Panna Cotta

Servings: 5-6 small ramekins

Prep Time: 15 min.

Chill Time: 4 hours

Ingredients:

2 c. half and half

1 tsp. vanilla

½ c. Greek yogurt

¾ c. confectionary sugar

2 tsp. kosher gelatin

2 tsp. water

Pomegranate Glaze:

¼ c. De La Rosa pomegranate vinegar

¼ c. pomegranate juice

¼ c. sugar

fresh pomegranate seeds

Directions:

1. Warm the half and half, confectionary sugar and vanilla in a saucepan. Sprinkle the gelatin over the water until softened. Add the gelatin to the saucepan and heat until dissolved. Take the saucepan off the heat and stir in the yogurt.
2. Pour the mixture into 5 or 6 small ramekins and chill for 4 hours or until set. In a saucepan, heat the De La Rosa pomegranate vinegar, pomegranate juice and sugar until boiling. Let it reduce on a low flame for 10 minutes until it becomes a syrupy consistency. Drizzle over the panna cotta and serve with fresh pomegranate arils. Enjoy!

*The pomegranate glaze can be enjoyed over cheesecake or blintzes as well.

*The kosher gelatin can be found on Amazon.com, as well as the De La Rosa pomegranate vinegar.

Pomegranate Panna Cotta

Acai Bowls

Servings: 3-4

Prep Time: 5 min.

Ingredients:

2 frozen acai packets (I use Sambazon, available in Wegman's or BJ's)

2 frozen bananas

½ c. fresh checked strawberries

½ c. fresh checked blueberries

water or milk, for thinning

Toppings:

Store-bought granola

flaked coconut

almond butter

blueberries, bananas, or strawberries

chocolate chunks

Directions:

1. Puree the acai packets with the frozen bananas and strawberries and blueberries in the blender. Use milk or water to thin the mixture to the desired consistency.
2. Pour into a bowl and top with your favorite toppings.

Acai Bowls

No-Bake Cheesecake Bites

Servings: One Dozen

Prep Time: 10 min.

Ingredients:

8 oz. whipped cream cheese

10 honey graham crackers, crushed

1 tsp. vanilla extract

¼ c. sugar

1 milk chocolate bar

1 white chocolate bar

1 tsp. coconut oil

Crushed cookies, nuts, or sprinkles for topping

Directions:

1. Mix the cream cheese, crushed graham cracker crumbs, vanilla and sugar.
2. Form into round balls and place on parchment paper. Freeze until firm.
3. Microwave the white and milk chocolate together with the coconut oil for 1-2 min.
4. Dip the cheesecake balls into the chocolate mixture and top with toppings. Freeze until ready to serve.

Cheesecake Bites

Think Pink

Servings: 2

Ingredients:

8 large frozen strawberries

2 c. grape juice

7.5 oz ginger ale

2 cups Rose wine

Directions:

1. Blend the strawberries and grape juice together in a blender. Fill the pureed strawberries on the bottom of two glasses.
2. Top with the ginger ale and Rose.

Iced Nanade

Servings: 2

Ingredients:

1 Wissotzky Nana Mint teabag

2 tbsp. honey

12 oz. water

12 oz. sweetened lemonade

Directions:

1. Pour boiling water in a 12 oz. hot cup. Add the honey and teabag. Allow the tea to steep for 15 min. Discard the teabag and freeze the tea in the cup.
2. Pop the frozen tea into the blender with the lemonade, and blend. For an optional alcoholic twist, add a little rum or tequila.

Think Pink

Iced Nanade

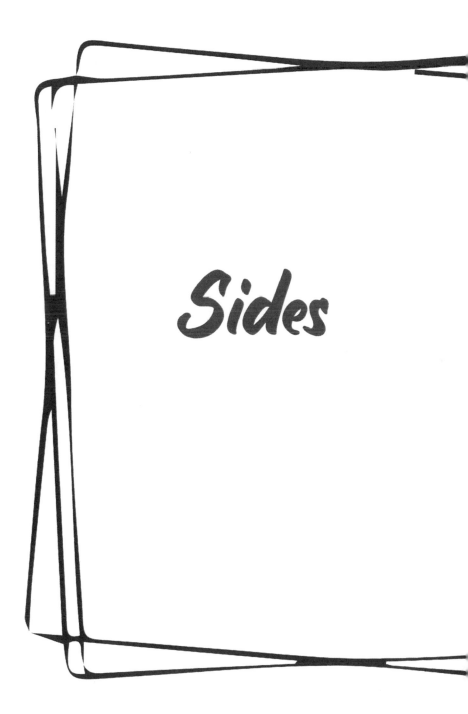

Sides

Roasted Carrots with Tahini Drizzle

Servings: 4

Prep Time: 5 min.

Cook Time: 30 min.

Ingredients:

1 lb. multi-colored carrots

olive oil

2 Tbsp. Trader Joe's Chili Lime spice

2 Tbsp. silan

1 Tbsp. paprika

1 Tbsp. garlic powder

1 container prepared techina

1 bunch checked parsley

Directions:

1. Peel the carrots. Drizzle with olive oil and toss in the spices. Place the carrots in a pan and roast in the oven on 400 for about a half hour or until done.
2. Drizzle with the prepared techina and top with parsley.

Roasted Carrots with Tahini Drizzle

Warning: These are addictive. Crispy, crunchy and salty, they are the ultimate snack. Serve them inside a salad, in a wrap, as a side-dish, or just snack on them alone.

Chili-Lime Crunchy Chickpeas

Servings: 4

Prep Time: 5 min.

Cook Time: 15-20 min.

Ingredients:

2 cans chickpeas

1 lime

1 Tbsp. Trader Joe's Chili-Lime Seasoning

1 tsp. Lawry's Garlic Salt

1 Tbsp. paprika

1 Tbsp. garlic powder

canola cooking spray

Directions:

1. Preheat the oven to 425. Drain the chickpeas well, then blot them with paper towels until they are dry.
2. Spray a shallow 9 by 13 pan or cookie sheet. Spray the chickpeas with cooking spray and then coat in the spices. Squeeze the juice of a lime over the chickpeas.
3. Cook for 15-20 minutes until roasted and crunchy. Enjoy!

Chili-Lime Crunchy Chickpeas

Bacon Corn Muffins

Servings: 1 dozen muffins

Prep Time: 10 min.

Cook Time: 30 min.

Ingredients:

1 package "kosher bacon"

cayenne pepper

maple syrup

1 c. flour

1 c. cornmeal

1 tsp. baking powder

½ c. sugar

2 eggs

¼ c. maple syrup

¼ c. melted Smart Balance or

margarine 1 c. parve almond milk

Directions:

1. Spray a cookie sheet and lay the bacon flat. Drizzle maple syrup on top and sprinkle a little cayenne pepper. Bake at 425 degrees Fahrenheit until crispy.
2. Meanwhile, mix the dry ingredients. Add the eggs, maple syrup, melted Smart Balance, and almond milk.
3. Crush the bacon into little pieces and add it to the batter. Any melted fat from the pan should be added to the batter, as well.
4. Place into greased muffin tins and bake at 400 degrees Fahrenheit for about 15-20 minutes. Enjoy!

Bacon Corn Muffins

Roasted Purple Cabbage

Servings: 6

Prep Time: 5 min.

Cook Time: 35 min.

Ingredients:

1 purple cabbage

garlic powder

Trader Joe's Everything but the Bagel spice

salt and pepper

olive oil

Directions:

1. Cut the purple cabbage in round discs. Lay flat on a cookie sheet. Sprinkle the discs with garlic powder, salt and pepper. Shake generous amounts of Everything Spice over the cabbage.
2. Drizzle the cabbage with olive oil. Cook at 425 for around 30-35 minutes or until roasted.

Roasted Purple Cabbage

Breaded Tomatoes

Servings: 4

Prep Time: 5 min.

Cook Time: 30 min.

Ingredients:

6 plum tomatoes

1 tsp. garlic powder

1 tsp. paprika

1 tsp. oregano

1 tsp. Lawry's garlic salt

½ tsp. black pepper

Olive oil

Pereg "American" breadcrumbs

Directions:

1. Preheat the oven to 420. Cut the tomatoes in half, and place on a baking sheet.
2. Sprinkle the spices on top of the tomatoes and top each tomato with 1-2 Tbsp. of breadcrumbs.
3. Drizzle the tomatoes with a generous amount of olive oil and bake for 30 minutes.
4. Top with more oregano if desired.

Breaded Tomatoes

Desserts

Puffs with Tahini Cream and Nectarine Coulis

Servings: 6

Prep Time: 30 min.

Cook Time: 30 min.

Ingredients:

1 package puff-pastry dough

Smart Balance or margarine

cinnamon and Sugar

crushed shelled pistachios

Nectarine Coulis:

8 nectarines

2 c. water

1 cinnamon stick

1 tbsp. vanilla

½ c. sugar

Tahini Cream:

1 Rich's Whip

2 Tbsp. Tahini

Directions:

1. Cut the puff pastry into triangles. Brush with melted margarine or smart balance and sprinkle with cinnamon and sugar. Bake on a cookie sheet lined with parchment paper until done.
2. Slice the nectarines and add them to a saucepan. Add the sugar, cinnamon stick, water and vanilla. Simmer on low for a half hour or more, until the nectarines are tender and resemble an almost caramelized consistency.

3. Whip the Rich's Whip and add the tahini. Pour into a Ziploc or piping bag.
4. Serve the puff pastry cookies with the techina whip on top, nectarine coulis, and crushed pistachios.

Puffs with Tahini Cream and Nectarine Coulis

I love the hot and cold combo when it comes to desserts. I'll always order the runny chip or hot apple pie in a restaurant when it comes with a cold scoop of ice cream. I've combined my love of cookie butter with a hot, runny cake and the best part is...it takes five minutes! It's a gorgeous restaurant quality dessert made easy!

5 Ingredient Cookie Butter Lava Cakes

Servings: 4-5 small cakes

Prep Time: 10 min.

Cook Time: 15 min.

Ingredients:

1 c. Lotus cookie butter

2 c. powdered sugar

3 eggs

¼ c. water

1 bar of semi-sweet (parve) or milk chocolate

Directions:

1. In a bowl, mix the cookie butter and powdered sugar well with a spoon. Then, carefully add one egg at a time. Add the water and continue to mix until a batter is formed. Pour the batter halfway into four to five small oiled ramekins.
2. Add three pieces of chocolate into the middle of each ramekin. Cover the chocolate with the remaining batter. Bake at 425 degrees Fahrenheit for 15 minutes.

Cookie Butter Lava Cakes

Jam Bars

Servings: 1 dozen bars

Prep Time: 10 min.

Cook Time: 40 min.

Ingredients:

2 eggs

2/3 c. sugar

1 tsp. vanilla

¾ c. oil

¼ tsp. salt

3 cups flour

apricot jam

strawberry jam

Directions:

1. In a bowl, mix the eggs, sugar, vanilla, oil and salt. Gradually add the flour until a dough is formed. If the dough is too dry, add a little more oil until it is a good consistently. Take off a cup of dough and keep it in the freezer until needed.
2. Line a 9 by 13 pan with parchment paper. Press the dough down into the pan. Bake at 350 for 15 minutes, or until just baked. Spread the crust with a thick layer of apricot and strawberry jam. Take the cup of remaining dough out of the freezer and crumble on top of the jam.
3. Return to the oven and bake for an additional 25 minutes, or until the crust is golden and cooked through. Cut into bars and enjoy!

Jam Bars

I wanted to create a healthier version of a yummy treat for adults and kids to be enjoyed all year round. I had some black tahini in my home, and I wanted to test it out by incorporating it into chocolate coated date truffles. The nuttiness of the sesame adds a lot of depth to the dates and chocolate coating.

Black Tahini Truffles

Servings: One Dozen

Prep Time: 10 minutes

Ingredients:

14 oz. container of pitted medjool dates

¼ c. salted almonds

2 heaping tablespoons De La Rosa black sesame tahini

1 tablespoon shelled pistachios

Chocolate Shell Coating:

12 oz. vegan chocolate chips

3 tablespoons coconut oil

1 tablespoon black sesame tahini (I use De La Rosa)

crushed pistachios, for decorating

Directions:

1. In a food processor, blend the almonds, pistachios, tahini and dates together until a ball of a dough-like consistency is formed. Roll into small truffles and place on parchment paper. Freeze until firm.
2. Melt the vegan chocolate chips, coconut oil, and tahini until smooth. Dip the frozen date balls into the chocolate shell mixture and top with crushed pistachios.
3. Keep in the freezer until serving. Enjoy!

Black Tahini Truffles

I am not a fan of using raw eggs in my cooking. Although I love chocolate mousse, I used to refrain from making it because all the recipes called for eggs or egg whites. I would make a quick mousse out of whip and chocolate, but it wasn't the same thick consistency. I played around a lot until I discovered the beauty and versatility of coconut milk. This pie is so easy and delicious, and it also can be served on Pesach in a Kosher for Passover pie crust!

No-Bake Chocolate Mousse Pie

Servings: 8

Prep Time: 5 min.

Ingredients:

1 graham cracker pie crust

12 oz. chocolate chips

1 tsp. vanilla

1 can coconut milk

Optional Toppings:

marshmallows

Rich's Whip

fruit

crushed Viennese Crunch

Directions:

1. Heat the can of coconut milk over low heat until boiling. Pour on top of chocolate chips and let steep for a few minutes. Add the vanilla and mix until smooth and creamy. Pour into the pie crust. (For a S'mores version, top with marshmallows and broil for a few minutes until toasted.)
2. Refrigerate overnight until completely set. The mousse will be thick and creamy. Store in the fridge until serving.

No-Bake Mousse Pie

PB & CB Hamantaschen

Servings: 20 cookies

Prep Time: 45 min.

Cook Time: 15-20 min.

Ingredients:

2 eggs

½ c. sugar

½ c. oil

1 tsp. almond milk

2 c. flour

1/4 tsp. salt

½ tsp. baking powder

Filling:

¼ c. peanut butter

¼ c. cookie butter

Almond milk

Glaze:

cookie butter and boiling water

Directions:

1. In a big bowl, whisk the eggs, sugar, oil, and almond milk. Add the flour, baking powder, and salt until a smooth dough is formed. Refrigerate the dough for 30 minutes. Meanwhile, preheat the oven to 350. Make the filling by combining the cookie butter and peanut butter. If it's too thick, add some almond milk to thin it out to the desired texture.

2. Roll the dough out thinly on a floured surface and cut circle shapes using an upside-down glass. Put a spoonful of filling on each circle and pinch the dough tight into a triangular shape. Freeze the cookies for 15 minutes, then stick into the preheated oven. Bake for 15 minutes, or until golden brown.
3. Wait for the cookies to cool completely before drizzling them with the glaze. In a Styrofoam cup, pour some boiling water over cookie butter and mix until you get a glaze-like consistently. Pour the mixture into a Ziploc bag and snip off the bottom edge. Pipe the glaze over the hamantaschen. These freeze well and taste delicious! Enjoy!

Hamantaschen

Finally, I bring you my famous chocolate chip cookie recipe. No mixer, nothing fancy, just a bowl and spoon. It's perfect every time. There's a reason why it got into The Bais Yaakov of Baltimore cookbook. If you have no idea what I'm talking about, you didn't read my introduction.

Chewy Chocolate Chip Cookies

Servings: One Dozen

Prep Time: 10 min.

Cook Time: 10 min.

Ingredients:

2 c. flour

1 tsp. baking powder

¼ tsp. sea salt

1 c. light brown sugar

¾ c. white sugar

2 eggs

1 c. oil

1 bag semi-sweet chocolate chips

Directions:

1. In a large bowl, mix the sugar, flour, salt, and baking powder. Add the eggs and oil. Mix to combine.
2. Add the chocolate chips. Form small balls and place on parchment paper.
3. Bake at 350 for ten minutes ONLY. Even if they don't look fully done, take them out of the oven. Otherwise, they will not be chewy.
4. Allow them to rest for 5-10 minutes before eating or storing.

Chewy Chocolate Chip Cookies

Made in the USA
Middletown, DE
12 July 2020